CROCODILE CROSSING

by Schuyler Bull

Illustrated by Alan Male

*To the Talbots, for encouraging me to take the plunge, and to my
parents for understanding when I did —* S.B.

To my daughters, Sophie and Chloe — A.M.

Published by Soundprints Division of Trudy Corporation, Norwalk, Connecticut.

Book design: Marcin D. Pilchowski
Editor: Laura Gates Galvin
Editorial assistance: Chelsea Shriver

First Edition 2003
10 9 8 7 6 5 4 3 2 1
Printed in China

Acknowledgments:
  Our thanks to Michael Devlin of the Endangered Wildlife Trust for his curatorial review.

*Library of Congress Cataloging-in-Publication Data is
on file with the publisher and the Library of Congress.*

CROCODILE CROSSING

by Schuyler Bull
Illustrated by Alan Male

Soundprints
Where Children Discover...

A bright moon lights up the sky in Africa. In a patch of sandy soil, a mother crocodile waits for her eggs to hatch. She has been protecting her nest all winter. Tonight her wait is over!

Squeak! Chirp! Crack! Strange sounds come from under the sandy soil. The babies are hatching!

Mother Crocodile paws at the earth, uncovering the eggs. Her hatchlings are coming out of their shells. By morning, nearly fifty baby crocodiles are hatched.

Mother Crocodile gently scoops up some of the babies in her mouth and carries them to a small pool nearby. She makes many trips back and forth until all the babies are safe in the water.

In the morning, one of the babies catches his first meal—a water bug!

After his breakfast, the baby croc watches a fish swimming back and forth in the water. The curious baby follows the fish. But when the baby croc gets too close, the fish turns and chases him away!

All afternoon, the crocodiles float in the pool while the sun beats down on them.

It is now June. It has not rained for weeks. There are no more bugs in the pool for the crocodiles to eat. Mother Crocodile must move her family to the Luangwa River.

Hurrying her family to the river, Mother Crocodile suddenly thrashes off the path, her large jaws snapping wildly. The baby crocs run for cover. A hungry marabou has been stalking the babies from the tall grasses nearby!

The bird flies away. Mother Crocodile's babies are safe. They continue their journey.

Finally, the crocodiles reach the river. There are other crocodiles at the river, too. The baby crocodiles wait as their mother slowly steps into the water.

The river is filled with activity—birds fly in and out of their nests to catch insects, rhinos dive into the water for a quick bath and storks hunt for small fish and clams.

The babies watch Mother Crocodile before sliding into the water. They then begin their own search for bugs and fish. One young croc paddles to the far end of the river. Suddenly, he hears the call of an eagle!

The baby croc cries out and dives under the water. *Splash!* The hungry bird follows!

The baby crocodile rises to the surface and sees the eagle again. This time, the bird has a catfish in his talons. He has found an easier meal than the baby croc. Instantly, Mother Crocodile appears. She quickly leads the young croc toward the shore.

Now safe, the young croc watches the eagle fly up to its nest, lugging the heavy fish along with it.

The young croc tumbles and plays with his brothers and sisters. One young croc sits on Mother Crocodile's head!

The young crocodiles watch as a male crocodile makes his way toward some zebras drinking along the water's edge. Three large crocodiles follow.

Soon, the crocodiles are almost nose-to-nose with the herd. Suddenly, the largest crocodile leaps from the water and tries to grab a zebra. The herd runs to safety.

During the drought, many animals along the river cannot find food. But the crocodiles are more successful.

One morning, a large crocodile finds a meal big enough for all the crocodiles, including Mother Crocodile and her family. They all take turns eating until everyone has had some food.

In the afternoon, the sun beats down on the dry land. Mother Crocodile moves her family to the water to escape the heat. She opens her mouth wide to cool herself. A small plover darts in and out of her giant mouth, cleaning her teeth. From the muddy shore, Mother Crocodile watches her young crocodiles in the river.

A few days later, the rain finally comes!
At night, the crocodiles pull themselves
onto the banks of the river. Animal calls echo
through the brush around the river. It is cool
and clear in the fresh new grasses where the
crocodiles sleep. The silver moon rises above
them and shimmers down over the flowing
waters of the Luangwa River.

THE NILE CROCODILE LIVES IN SOUTHERN AFRICA

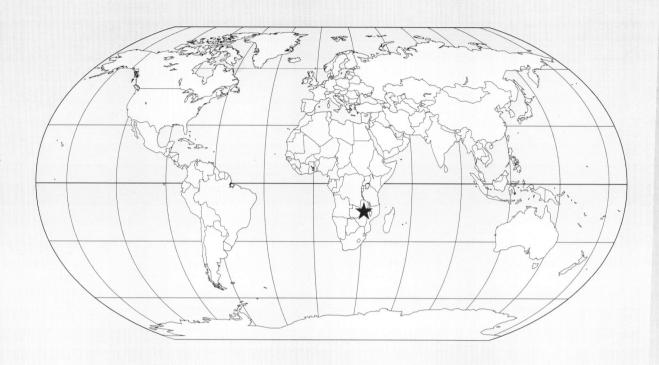

ABOUT THE NILE CROCODILE

Nile crocodiles live mostly around rivers, marshes and lakes in southern Africa. There are almost no Nile crocodiles in the Nile River of Egypt today. They have been around for over 70 million years!

Some people confuse crocodiles with alligators. Crocodiles have long, pointed snouts, while alligators have shorter, rounded snouts. Crocodiles also have many special features that help them survive in the wild. They have sharp teeth, very tough skin and the ability to float or sink whenever they want.

Crocodiles eat almost anything—fish, turtles, crustaceans, baboons, hyenas and wildebeest—just to name a few! A crocodile's jaws do not move sideways, so they cannot chew their food. Instead, they rip off a piece of food and swallow it whole.

Crocodiles grow to be as long as 20 feet and can weigh as much as 2,000 pounds. They usually live about forty-five years.

Crocodiles have highly developed brains, making them the smartest of all reptiles!